I

It was one hundred years ahead into future. Nobody had lived to tell this story, so I, Willa Willianna, the latest and greatest only commanding head official of the Federal Department of Water Regulations, shall speak from the mass grave that was dug up before all the humans of this planet perished due to the Great Drought.

So far, I was the one and only commanding leader of the Federal Department of Water Regulations. Believe you me, I died umpteenth times over, but due to the ability to cryogenically freeze, I had been able to return countless and countless of times. This time was different, though, because there was no one to freeze me. The ability to cryogenically freeze was not the stuff of movies; it had been tested underground in a top-secret location for military purposes (very hush-hush) since the turn of the new millennium (twentieth-first century).

Ever since this crisis over the drought, which began in the early years of the twentieth-first century, I had been trying to work to regulate the flow of the water, known to many the common folks as the ‘cause,’ as the title of the new department called for. My duties were to regulate people’s usage of their water supply due to the impending drought. I even studied water regulation at university. It was my main goal in life-in *everyone’s* life, as a matter of fact-that we lived to see another day, *with* water. In order to do that, we *must* conserve water, no matter the cost in livelihood. We cannot die of dehydration; we just *cannot*! Somehow, someway, we will come out of this drought alive! We will make it through or die tryin’!

Due to the drought that started one hundred years ago, the world, as we knew it, no longer existed, not even for zombies or werewolves because they fed off of other living humans and humans were dying off as we speak. Because no other living species existed, they, too, died off. No living soul remained; they became extinct due to dehydration cause by lack of water.

Before the Great Drought, the whole world was in a terrible, horrible global warming crisis, which, in turn, succumbed into the greatest drought we knew ever existed in the history of this world, turning our world into desert wasteland known as the aforementioned Great Drought. People were already dying out by the *dozens* due to lack of water as I mentioned before since they *lived* on the stuff. Slowly, they became dehydrated. People who were most susceptible to dehydration were little kids, who loved to be active, and athletes. Elderlies also were dehydrated quickly. These were one of the first demographics to perish. This environment was not for the faint of heart, sad to say.

Since early millennium of the twentieth-first century in 2015, the whole world had started becoming a desert wasteland because it had not rained for *five whole years*!!! However, it had not happened overnight. You cannot control the weather, but you *can* control what you eat. People started finding liquid from *other* sources like fruits and dairy products, but they *needed* water! They continued making smoothies, milkshakes and malts. They became inventive, making lactose-free milkshakes and smoothies that tasted like water. But, still, it was not enough! People became less healthier and more obese; the life expectancy started to lower, no matter *how many* cosmetic surgeries they had done to themselves. They still seemed gross. Nobody even had the effort to go to the gym; the minute they went, they still ended up gaining it *right on back*!!!

Another way I had of conserving water was not allowing people to build bathrooms in their private residences. Also, businesses were not allowed to build bathrooms for public usage. People had to wear diapers instead of going to the bathrooms. The diapers they used were disposable, cloth ones like the ones for babies when people went camping.

In order to conserve water, people were allowed to take showers and/or baths, wash their cars and/or pets once a month. But they were underhanded. They took showers and/or bath very late at night. They also washed their cars and/or pets late at night. People were violating a *hundred* laws due to the Federal Department of Water Regulations, so I set up a Water Unit at every single police station in America! First, it started in America, and then it started to catch on. Then it went global. I knew when people started using water consumption, according to my Water Tracker Device that tracked every single household's water usage in America. People in other countries wanted to use my Water Tracker Device, so I invented some more, but I kept the original for our usage. (Besides being a water conservator, I was also *quite* an inventor!) People's water usage was mainly late at night.

The water tanks that people use for water and sanitation could not be used anymore because of the drought. Therefore, the resources became depleted as the drought dragged *on and on*! People and their material goods were not cleaned for *days on end*! When it rained, however, it was like a luxury like no other, but it would not last. When one person was not clean, it meant she or he was mentally unstable. But when the whole *world* was not clean, it meant everybody was in the same ill-begotten boat.

By 2025, nowhere in the world rain anywhere, not even for people who grew fruits and vegetables or for farm animals. Not even a *single* drop of rain!!! So there were lack of smoothies and milkshakes.

Farm animals became so thin and ugly that no one would want to buy them. Even if the farmers sold them, city folks would not want to eat gross food! At first, people were happy to lose the weight, but then they became emaciated like the people in Africa during the famine. So emaciated they were, their *bones* were showing through their clothes, a stranger might have thought they were anorexia or bulimic. Turned out, everyone was this way. I felt terrible that I passed all those laws, restricting them from those fun-filled days before the Great Drought struck. Looking back, I thought I was doing the world good by conserving water, but I think I had overdone it.

Speaking of farming, there was a lack of water for homegrown fruits and vegetables even for suburban gardens. Also, there was no water at all for the surburbanites' front lawns, never mind their backyard vegetable gardens. All their vegetations wilted to nothingness, including their lawn, which were overgrown with dry weeds and other plants. Bugs and other pesticides eat at their plants, making them inedible.

Not only farming was not available due to lack of water supply, but any sign of forests or any floral life for miles and miles around was not apparent. People may have thought redwoods would have lived millions and millions years. But due to lack of water, they perished during the Great Drought. The Amazon Rainforest was amongst one of the victims of the Great Drought. These and many more forests and great national parks of the United States and international parks of the world were decimated because of the Great Drought, not due to some man-made catastrophe like an accidental fire. Sometimes people forget to put out their fire after camping or throwing out their cigarette butts out the window passing by a certain national forest. Even worse yet, most men were causing deforestation clearing the woods of their beautiful trees before nature caused it to run its well run dry of water, so to speak.

Then came the Great Drought in which all the national forest parks of the United States and international forest parks of the world began to disappear due to lack of water. Slowly at first, but then as the years went by, no rain occurred for years on end that people and animals and even plant life eventually forgot what rainwater felt like that they begun dying off. Slowly, the plants wilted. AFFgnimals were dying off right and left, no matter how much they stored up; it was not enough.

As the animals began dying off, forests too look terrible. It looked like had been maintaining it for eons, but the fact of the matter was, it had not been raining for what seemed like an eternity.

Either way, it did not matter much now anyways. People visited national parks much anymore, so with that in mind, parks ending up being closed. Park rangers ended up losing their jobs, but the forests continued to look a mess.

Forests looked like it could be found on an episode of *Twilight Zone*, where everything was deteriorating to the point of no return. Lakes were drying up. Animals' carcasses were found on the side of the road; sometimes right in the middle of the road. Roadkill alert! But nobody killed them; they just died off due to lack of water. The once-lively forests were dead.

In this terribly sad world, no one lasted a *week* because there was nothing any more to subsist on. The first two groups to go first were the youngest, the littlest babes, who had such a short existence on this planet, (So sad. What a waste!) and the feeble, oldest elderly, who had already enjoyed a long and happy life, had to die in such a tragic way. For the young, everyday I blamed myself till I, too, drew the last breath. For the old, I deprived them of living their last moments on earth in harmony and of watching their grandchildren getting married and having their own beautiful children.

For the young, I should not have restricted them for the joys having a couple of smoothies or milkshakes. For the elderly, I wish they had the chance to see their grandbabes grow up, but I deprive that joy. It was all my fault! I thought bitterly to myself as I watched them leave this world.

The strong adults, both in mind and spirit, lasted a little bit longer. They helped the physically and mentally weak. But they, too, were getting weaker as each day passed by. Not one day passed by that they wanted more to subsist on.

They dreamt of days passed when they had plenty. Days when they realized there was a future. I was one of them because I thought I might come back again. Later, as I thought about it, I came to the realization that no one will cryogenically freeze me this time around.

I was one of the last to go. I was one of the many strong-willed. I helped care for the weak. Although I was the leader, it was times like these that it was time to test our faith in each other. Everybody was his or her own leader. They each follow their own instincts. We worked as a team, incorporating our gifts together. When it was time for our patients to leave this world and cross over to the other side, we gave them a proper send-off, with tears in our eyes even though it was the same each and every time.

It was hard on me each and every time because my parents had already passed on. They were one of the many elderlies who had died during the Great Drought. They were centenarians, so they were unlikely to have last long through the Great Drought, but, still, it was sad when they passed on.

Some people who had already given up were those kids' parents. They lived for those kids. They based their whole lives on their kids' whole existence, however short it was. After their little ones had passed on, they thought there was nothing to live for. They might have attempted suicide, but after conferring with me, (I also had a degree in the medical field as well as one in law.), our team of hospital workers talked them down, giving them a sedative if they became too agitated. Most of the time we put them on suicide watch. Even though sometimes our team, too, felt like giving up, we plowed right on through every single obstacle standing in our way.

Other people who had just about given up were caregivers of their elderly parents, who suddenly died almost overnight, sometimes for no apparent reason. Here they were caring for this individual practically since they had entered their twilight years, and they suddenly died for no apparent reason. That was kind of frustrating, to say the least. The caregiver would talk to one of our counselors or somebody else in that field like a social worker.

Now back to the water crisis at hand. At first, the ponds dried up. But nobody noticed because hardly anyone went to the ponds. But then they started seeing dead ducks in the ponds. I started the Water Unit at the police departments, shortened to the Water Police, all across the country. The lines at the Water Unit were *ringing off the hook*! But *nothing* at all was being done about it! It was a higher priority that people were dying of dehydration instead of *ducks* dying off, so they messaged the Federal Department of Water Regulations. Since I was in charge of the Federal Department of Water Regulations, they messaged me.

I checked up on the problem. You know what I discovered!? Not only were the ponds drying up, the *lakes* were also drying up! People can no longer fish there although they can quickly load up on the ish that were washed up ashore. They need not wait and wait for it. Since there was lack of lake water, it just laid there like they were waiting to be caught. Smart 'fishermen' used a harpoon to grab a whole load of fishes and load it in their cooler. What a catch! What a catch!

People were catching ducks, too. You know, they were too cute to eat. But there was nothing *else* to eat since cows, chickens and other kinds of land animals were too sickly-looking to buy from the country bumpkins. And 'sides, they were sitting ducks anyways.

On the other hand, corpses of long-dead people came floating up to the surface. Dozens upon dozens of bodies floated to the surface. Cold cases were solved, but the killers were still at-large.

Or maybe they were dead. But after I discovered the bodies, I sent the case to the Federal Bureau of Investigation (FBI).

The rivers were drying up, which caused alligators and crocodiles to come washing ashore. First, locals took the once-wild beasts' teeth, so sharp they were! Now they looked so *pathetic*!. People were saying, "Spineless creatures! Not so tough anymore, are you now?" After people took their once-scary and dangerous teeth they started greedily taking pieces of these river animals to eat.

Weeks passed by. People who went to the beach very often noticed something strange. They noticed the water reached as far as it usually did; they had to go further to get into the water. A month or two passed by when the surfers noticed they had to go very, very far to catch a wave, if there even *was* a wave to catch that day, which rarely so much as happened nowadays.

Not only people cannot swim, snorkel, surf or do any other water activities no longer, sea life was being washed ashore like in the ponds and lakes. In the beginning, it was little-bitty fishes that people normally fished for although there were an unusual mixture of clams and mollusks, starfishes and school of fishes, plus a scattering of sea plant life like coral reef and seaweed. Then there were jellyfishes and scorpions and stingrays, however poisonous they were, people just grabbed them up because they were dead anyways, so how poisonous could they be? But first, they took the stinger out.

At first, people, especially beachcombers and fishermen, enjoyed getting their load of fishes and other ocean life. Then when the bigger fishes like whales and sharks came along, they realized they had a *big* problem on their hands. Big fishes started washing ashore. People had seen a beached whale before but never had they seen a beached shark. It was a both a surprising and startling sight. Sharks looked ten million times meaner than a whale, though it was the same size as a whale. They could not get the whales and sharks back into the ocean because the water was receding, little by little each day. People took full advantage of these big fishes being washed ashore.

First, they took the blubber from the whales and the shark fins from the sharks so sharp they were! Now they looked so *pathetic*! People, far and wide, came to look at it, prodding at it, saying, "Ha, ha! You are not so tough after all! You pathetic, worthless piece of thing!" They then began greedily taking pieces of these big ocean animals to eat.

On the other hand, the corpses of the murdered victims whose bodies were dropped into their watery graves were washed up from the receding ocean. The beachgoers who found the bodies were so traumatized but not so traumatized that they were able to call the local authorities.

They reported this to the Coast Guard, who did so much as twitch an eyebrow, going, "Nothing *we* can do about that, miss. Report it to the Federal Department of Water Regulations, if you want."

So I had to hear from the beachgoers via email that the ocean was now receding. Here was the email:

Dear Willa Willianna:

From itty-bitty fishes like shellfishes to huge fishes like whales and sharks, fishes are being washed ashore over by the local ocean we frequent. This is because the ocean is now receding. You have to go very far in order to swim. Speaking of water activities, you can no longer snorkel, surf or even jet-ski because the water is receding. We can no longer enjoy the beach as we once used to.

But one thing that irks me-that irks us, beach lovers-is the way all those long-dead murder victims suddenly wash ashore take away our joy of our beachgoing experience.

We kindly beseech you to do something about it, please. Thank you for your time.

A beach lover

Even though the email was unsigned, it said where it was sent from. I sent an email back to ask if this was some kind of a prank. To which the reply was, "*The previous email is not a hoax. You ought to check out the situation, Ms. Willianna.*"

I finally decided to put my trust on the emailer against my better judgment, so I took a plane out to California, where the email had come from. (I had one of my detective friends traced the email to California.)

When I got to San Francisco, my hometown, I got all misted-eyed. I had not been back here since I left for university. Anyways, I decided to check out Ocean Beach, my favorite beach haunt or what *used* to be Ocean Beach. As soon as I got there, I had not seen the beach anywhere in sight. All I saw was sand. Sand everywhere - all over but *no water*! The 'beach' was empty, and it was a perfectly beautiful day. *So it is true,*

I thought, *what has been happening to the ocean! What are we gonna do about it?*

This world was turning into a desert. No water. There had not been any kind of fruits or vegetables to get any kind of water from. People were dying right and left of dehydration. They were seriously lacking in water.

As I was turning these thoughts round and round in my head, a 'beach' bum suddenly came out of nowhere and beseeched me drunkenly, "Horney, wha ha been happening to dis beach?!

Tell me!" I can smell his dirty, beachy smell and see his rotting, yellow teeth. In his hand, he carried a bag of liquor. Being close to him caused me to feel nauseated. Since apparently he was the only person around to answer my questions, I asked him the most pertinent questions.

Despite my better judgment, I asked him, "What happened to the water?"

After he took a swig from the paper bag, spilling some brown liquor onto the sand, he said, slurring his words, "De water one day shlowly but shurely disappear. Even de fishes ended up on de shore."

As soon as he shuffled away, drinking from the paper bag, I threw up right onto the sand. *Oh my God,* I thought as I bent forth with my hands on my knees, puking my guts out. *Is this what we have come to? Relying on bums for information on the state of our planet?*

Finally, I wiped my mouth on my sleeve and buried my puke underneath all that sand and then I got my composure back. But even though it really was not necessary, I put some lip gloss on, which made me feel a teensy-bit better. I straightened my posture, looked around and saw a beach house nearby. I decided to go and inquire them about the disappearing ocean.

I went onto the deck and knocked and knocked on the sliding glass door, but no one answered, so I peered into the door. It apparently looked empty. There were no furniture, no electronic gadgets, no nothing. It looked like nobody lived there. Stuck in the fireplace was what looked like some kind of furniture or something like that. Apparently, they were turning the furniture into firewood. I found that the door was unlocked, so I invited myself in. Upon further investigation, I discovered two adult skeletons and two child skeletons. *They must have wasted away due to lack of water,* I thought sadly.

I went onto the next house, where I discovered practically the same sad state of affairs. So I decided to go to the local police station to report this. But when I got there, it was unusually quiet for a police station. No cops were coming in or going out with their arrested criminals. It was so *unbelievably* quiet that nobody would have known it was a police station. *It cannot be.* I thought. *They cannot all be dead. Only one way to find out.*

So I went on up inside the police station, and my worst fears were confirmed: everyone had perished in the Great Drought. Not a living soul escaped this catastrophe – except maybe for that beach bum I saw maybe what seemed like eons ago. *Oh, whatever shall I do? Are we the last living souls on this planet? Oh, the bane of our existence!* I exited the police station and walked to the residential area, where my family house once was.

When I reached my old childhood neighborhood, I saw a an in incredible sight! I saw a young family exiting from an old bomb shelter that was used during air raids in the World Wars period. *Huh?* I thought. *I never knew they have bomb shelters in San Francisco. What are they doing there?* As I continued watching them while hiding between two port-a-potty, I saw them go back into their house.

They were not the only family in that neighborhood that came out of a bomb shelter. In other neighboring houses, there were more people of various ages from young to old coming out of bomb shelters with bottles of various sizes filled with water. *Where did they get all that water?* I wondered.

One house I stopped at was so loud and boisterous I could hear them from the sidewalk! The loudest of the bunch, which I guessed was the leader of the gang, said, "We got them *good*! There is a spring under Golden Gate Bridge that *no one* knows about! It'll never, *ever* dry up!"

To which his friends said, "Cheers to spring water!"

It was quiet for a moment. Then he said, "Of *course* it is legal. It is our own water! Don't be silly!"

Since this neighborhood was filled with the last of the last remaining people in the country as far as I knew, I decided to go in search of the spring underneath the Golden Gate Bridge. I walked really fast away from the partiers. When I had past by their house, I ran pell-mell down the street, my shoes slapping hard against the concrete pavement. By the time I reached the Golden Gate Bridge, my legs were ready to fall off because there was no transportation of any sort because gasoline prices were sky-high. Besides, local transportation like Muni and BART did not even exist anymore. They also needed gasoline, and gasoline was a form of liquid, which had become a rarity. Only the rich were allowed that kind of luxury.

I took a break by the once-bustling tourist trap, Pier 39, but it was no longer. Apparently, no one had visited this area in eons because it looked so deserted. No kids, tourists, no sign of life anywhere for *miles* around! Not even a gum or candy wrapper around. It had become a sad, desolate place.

After a few moments had passed by, and I had rested my poor, blistered feet, I got up and went on ahead to the Golden Gate Bridge, where, to my surprise, there were no more cars swishing back and forth on it. There were also no more pedestrians on the walkway. On my way over here from my old neighborhood, I had not seen any people except for the people in my old neighborhood. Not one living soul. Kind of gave me the chills. *How could it be?* I thought. *Are we the last of the last?*

Quickly, I refocused my attention back to the solution at hand: to locate the spring. I went underneath the Golden Gate Bridge, where it was all but dry up, filled with suicidal bodies that had jumped off the Golden Gate Bridge. *What are they, kidding me?* I thought. *There's no spring here!*

Upon closer observation, I saw that the dead bodies that piled in two separate piles. There was a pile on the left and one on the right. In the center, water was spurting out. "*Eureka!*" I yelped. "*So this is where the spring is!*"

I took my empty canister out of my camping pack and filled it to the brim. Then I took all of my empty containers and filled them with water. *Ah,* I thought, *Fresh spring water!*

After I took a gratifying swallow, I was able to think better on my feet. I thought, *I could harness this water for others who are incapable of finding their own resources.*

I dug around some more. I was not afraid to get my hands a little dirty. The spring had sprung, so to speak. *But,* I figured, *it must lead somewheres.* After digging for what seemed like an eternity, I hit jackpot! Deep, deep beneath all that dirt was water! Oh, it felt so glorious beneath my bare skin!

I emptied all of the containers that I had not previously yet filled into my satchel so that I can fill it up with water. After I filled every single one of my containers with fresh water, I set out for the hospitals filled with plentiful surplus of water supply. But first, I recovered the water with dirt so that no one else will get at it.

At every single hospital, I went to they were very much appreciated, but they all wanted to know where and how I got the water because they wanted to get it for themselves. To which I replied, "I'm the water supplier. Let me worry about it, okay? You just worry about saving lives."

After people begun drinking the Golden Gate Bridge water, they started to become hydrate once again. They started to become more alive, body and soul. They started requesting me for more water. More, more, more!!!! That was all they wanted of me!!! They started to drive me to the brink of insanity!

I had no future plans to go back to my job in Washington D.C. as the head of Federal Department of Water Regulations. I am pretty much sick and tired of that job. I decided to live out the rest of my days in the once-bustling tourist trap Pier 39 right near Golden Gate Bridge. It was now practically deserted. No loud ringing of arcade. No locals or tourists passing by. Just an empty pier. Oh, I looted the tourist attractions, looking for remnants of food or whatnot. Sometimes I found it; sometimes not. One time, I found a stale piece of sourdough bread at Boudin's where I was staying. Another time I found an old stale burger from the big McDonald's on Fisherman's Wharf. All of the food I found was stale but still rather edible.

Anyways, when I discovered one of my so-called 'patients' were stalking me, I switched up my temporary residence to the Aquarium of the Bay, where plenty of animals still lived there. I decided to live there amongst the fishes and other marine life as well.

I used to go to Pier 39 as a kid with my friends. It was so much fun! Now I found it to be lonesome without anyone to keep me company (except for the fishes) and to people-watch. I especially enjoyed people-watching so that I can ridicule those tourists who come to Pier 39 for the very first time with a whole new perception of things.

I also wondered what it would be like to have a whole new perception of things from a different point of view.

Now I knew. I knew what was it liked to feel lonesome in this scary world, where there was no one you can depend on but yourself.

Maybe once a month, I bathe in the water. I loaded up my canister with water and bathe in it. I knew water was still in short supply like gold or silver back in the day, so I tried to conserve as much as I can. But after I loaded my canister with water, I striped down and poured water all over my head. I would not even wash my hair till the end of the month.

I realized I had not wanted things to change till too late. I liked things the way it was going, but sometimes things had a way of coming out in the open. One day as I was doing my usual looting or, rather, 'browsing,' somebody saw me lurking around. It so happened to be one of my former 'patients.' "Hey, you!" said the man. "Whatchu doin' in my store?!" I was guessing he had not recognized me since I saved his live.

"I am just looking around, sir," I said meekly, hands in the arms in defense, backing out of the store. "In my defense, I did not know anyone was in here. So sorry, mister."

"Hey, Ms. Kleptomaniac!" yelled out the store manager. "Did you lift anything from my store? Empty your pockets, miss! Right now!"

"*Why?*" I muttered under my breath in protestation. "*Why, oh, why did I ever get caught?*"

My pockets were filled with various junk acquired while Pier 39 was empty. My denim jacket pockets were filled with crumpled-up gum and candy wrappers. I mostly just kept the tinfoil gum wrappers. I loved soft candy. I loved saving Bazooka comics, which I had collected folded neatly in a Ziploc bag. There was also an old, purple, discolored (you could not even tell that it once used to be purple; it was now grey) yo-yo that my older brother Cal had given me when I was nine as a birthday present right before he went off to Iraq, then to Afghanistan and never came back; that was the only memento I had of him. I had kept as a keepsake, but it had not work for a long time now because the string had broke. And let's not forget about my Swiss army knife with a pair of folding scissors and a can opener. It had its standard knife contraption. It also had a nail clipper. It may be tight, but it still worked. I also had a few dirty tissues and napkins. Not to mention my leather wallet filled with its many credit cards and cash and other vital info.

"Okay, miss," said the man more calmly. "You are okay now. Sorry for calling you out."

"It is okay, mister. You were just doing your job," I said. "Just wondering: is everyone coming back yet?"

"Just about, miss," said the store manager. "Just about. We will open for business pretty soon. Oh,

I imagine," he said thoughtfully, stroking his beard. "In the coming days."

"Thanks a lot, mister!" I yelled, backing out of the souvenir shop. "I gotta run now!" I hurried back to where I had left my things in my hideaway at the Aquarium of the Bay to get my belongings and ditch the place before people started coming back. First the owners will be opening up their tourist attractions. Then the locals and tourists will be bringing back business to these establishments.

I took an Uber to the SFO where I bought a one-way ticket to Washington D.C., where the Federal Department of Water Regulations was located. Since I was away for waaaaaaay too long, they had given away my position as head official of the Federal Department of Water Regulations to someone else less competent than me, poor sap.

But I was able to infiltrate their camp since their techno system was weak and yet-to-be-updated because they were besieged with other viral problems in their cybersystem caused by hackers. They probably had given me up for dead since I had no communication with them in awhile. I was now a mere underling, not the head. I reported to the head whose name was Charley Angel; everyone referred to him as Angel.

Charley Angel's real name was Charles Angelito, but he preferred to be called Angel. He had a Latino background. His parents were Chicano. Back when he was teen in his hometown deep within South Central Los Angeles in Watts, California,he had joined a

Chicano gang, his so-called friends started calling him Angel, and it stuck. He left the gang when his family moved to Washington, D.C. and had a really great mentor, Angie Arrowhead, that gave him the motivation to acquire a federal job, working for the 'cause,' which was preventing the Great Drought before it happened, but it had already happened. Before meeting this mentor, he had no role model because both his parents were way too busy to give him the time of day. So busy, they practically forgotten he existed. Even after moving to the other side of the country, he was causing trouble when he again fell in with the wrong crowd, but thankfully, Ms. Arrowhead helped him out in his time of need. Not many people paid attention to him. She straightened him out.

Before working at the inner-city high school that Angel went and graduated from, she worked at a teen crisis clinic, free of charge. This clinic not only helped teens but tweens as well as young adults and disadvantaged that the system had overlooked. That was why she decided to work at Angel's school.

I reported to Angel that the water crisis was under control now on the West Coast. He checked it out on the Water Tracker Device that I myself invented. "Yup, it sure is. How did you do it?"

"Found a spring underneath Golden Gate Bridge," I said proudly.

"There is a spring under the Golden Gate Bridge!" he said in bewilderment.

"There *sure* is!" I exclaimed.

"Oh, I did not know," he said, stroking his beard. "But how will we pass out the water to the rest of the world?"

"I have not thought that far," I said. "We could put our heads together, but only if you allow me back on the team. Deal?"

"You got yourself a deal, Willa!" Angel said, shaking on it. "Why don't you sleep on it tonight? I will arrange an emergency board meeting tomorrow, okay?"

"*Okay, sir,*" I said, going back to my sublet.

In the morning, I woke up bright-eyed and bushy-tailed, so to speak, with a brilliant idea. It was like a light bulb went off in my head. I found blank spiral notebooks amongst my many spiral notebooks filled with half-baked plans and scrawls and other stuff and jotted down my plan.

At the Federal Building, I was hustled into the meeting room at the Federal Department of Water Regulations. At first, people were busily eating the pastries at the center of the conference room. But then, they noticed me. They were startled and surprised to see me back with them. So surprised and startled, they began mumbling and whispering amongst themselves.

It was good thing that Angel took charge. "As you all realized," he began, "Ms. Willianna is back with us."

There was a resounding applause all around the table. At first polite, then they were happily applauding.

"Moving along!" yelled Angel, getting everyone's attention, waving his hands for silence. "As y'all know, I was just her temporary replacement until she got back, but now that she is back, I would like y'all you to give her your full and undivided attention please."

With that, Angel moved over and gave up the podium over to me.

"*Thank you, all, for that reception. I am happy to be back. Now let's get down to business,*" getting all business-like.

"*Now when I went to the West Coast to check on things, I discovered that the ocean was disappearing,*" I said.

"Tell me something I *don't* know," muttered a cocky guy named Bruce Collins.

Choosing to ignore him, I went on, "*Well, when I went back to my old neighborhood, I discovered that people were well supplied with–guess what?–water!*"

People around the table started looking quizzically at each other. "***Huh? What? Where did they get the water?***" they were mumbling to each other.

"If you wanna know where they got the water, here it is," I said. "From a spring underneath the Golden Gate Bridge! It is all credited to the people from my childhood neighborhood."

"So how do you suggest we bring the water supply to the others in the world?" asked Bruce, who always found a reason to show how incompetent I was at my job.

Slowly, I turned towards him with a condescending smile on my face. I had never had any trouble being condescending towards him. "*Well, Brucie boy, I have figured all that out.*" I knew it irked him to call him 'Brucie boy,' but I did it anyways, just to annoy him.

Turning to everyone else, I continued, "*We could put the water we found from the* spring in one of those chemtrail planes. Instead of spraying chemicals, we could spray water into farms and forests, both international and national."

"Great idea!" said Angel, clapping his hands, which everybody then followed suit, but Bruce was the only one who did not clap.

"Brava!" said Bruce quite sarcastically. "Brava!"

"You have something to say, Bruce?" I asked.

"If you have this idea, why did it take you so long to come back? Huh?" asked Bruce.

"Oh, that is not important," I said dismissively. "What's important is, I am here now, so let's get down to business. And another thing: We ought to set up water banks, in case of emergencies. You know how some hospitals have sperm banks and blood banks. Well, we can now have water banks for people who are dying of dehydration."

"That is a wonderful idea!" exclaimed Angel.

With that, everybody started cheering. Unnoticed, Bruce slunk out of there grumpily, passing the receptionist, who called after him, "What is going on in there, Mr. Collins?" to which he ignored. "What is *up* with you anyways?"

He did not speak till he left the building. After he had left the building, he lit up a cigarette. He mumbled under his breath, not swearing, per se, but more like bad-mouthing me, unbeknownst to me. We always kidded with each other, but it was not borderline hate. But Bruce always took things awfully seriously. He never partied; he did not even have much of a social life. He was a total and complete loner. He enjoyed being by himself. Life was much better that way.

He was this way because his family and friends betrayed him when he needed them the most. When he was diagnosed with Hodgkin's leukemia, he needed his family and friends, but they weren't there for him. He felt like they had betrayed him. He found fault in the universe everyday of his life! And I mean, *every single day*! That's why he was such a grumpy cat!

People oftentimes thought he was *born* grumpy with that permanent sour expression on his face; no one had ever, *ever* seen him with a friendly expression or heard him offer a kind word to anybody. Oh, people tried to joke him out of his grumpiness, but it just made him all the more sour! And then he would turn around and say something sarcastic. He either was called Sarcastic King or Grumpy the Cat, but what irked him the most was when I called him Brucie boy.

He most especially hated when I acted condescendingly towards him and smiled in my most condescending manner towards him. What he hated most of all was that a *woman* was in charge. He was some kind of male chauvinistic pig; gotta have the guy in charge or no go, so I just talked down to him.

When he had cooled down somewhat, he slipped back in unnoticed except by the receptionist, She was on the phone, so she was unable to greet him at all. She was used to his leaving the office abruptly by now, having worked in the office for five years now. She just nodded curtly at him as he passed by her and then went back to work.

Quietly and quickly, Bruce slipped back in unnoticed. The party was *still* going on. Half an hour had passed since he had stepped out for a smoke.

"*Alright, everybody!*" I called out. "*We have to put our plans into motion, okay?*"

They quieted down as they took their seats again although there was still some mumbling around the conference table. I paid them no heed and went ahead with my plan.

"Okay, everybody," I called, and they all quiet down. "Here is the plan: we could get the planes to spray water."

"But how will we get the planes' permission?" asked Bruce, skeptical.

Angel spoke up, "If it is for a worthy cause, those planes will let us use them for watering farms and forests even if it is not natural."

Angel rolled his eyes towards me, muttering under his breath, "There is always a skeptic. Always."

"You know, I can hear you, Angel," said Bruce, stretching out his name.

"Go on with your plan," said Angel to me, ignoring Bruce.

"We will also create water banks at hospitals from the Golden Gate Bridge Spring, which will help those that are dehydrated or dying of *dehydration,*" I went on, trying to ignore Bruce.

"How do you suggest we create water banks from a *spring* underneath the Golden Gate Bridge?" asked Bruce skeptically.

"*Well, Bruce, my dear,*" I said. "*I've thought and thought about this on my way back from San Francisco, and I came to the conclusion: the* mainstream water pipe can be directed from the Golden Gate Bridge Spring. We then affix water tubes to send the spring water to the water banks in the United States hospitals. Any more questions, Bruce? Or anyone else?"

"**I have a question,**" said a gruff-looking Latino named José.

"Yes, what is your question, José?" I asked.

"**How about the international hospitals?**" asked José.

"You know how the oceans are disappearing as we speak? Well, it will give us a leeway. By connecting these water tubes nationally, even internationally, we will be giving back not only our

planet, but also our people.

Yes, of course, we will be

connecting the water tubes

overseas," I said.

A young Chinese woman, who I didn't know her name, spoke up. "Sounds like a lot of work. Do we have enough in our budget to work with that much?"

"What is your name,

miss?" I asked

"My name?" she replied, pointing to herself. "My name's Sou-Yi."

"Well, Sou-Yi, are you willing to work for the 'cause'?" I asked.

"The 'cause'?" asked Sou-Yi, puzzled.

"The Great Drought," I replied.

"Yeah!" said Sou-Yi. "'Course I am!"

"*Then nothing matters till we defeat the Great Drought! Who is with me?!*" I roared. "*Everybody who is with me, shout 'Hell yeah!'*"

With that, everybody around the table shouted, "**HELL YEAH**!!!!" punching their fists in the air in unison even old skeptical Bruce.

After the meeting had dispersed, people left feeling so much happier than they had came in, looking towards a brighter and more optimistic future, leaving Angel and me alone in the conference room.

Angel said to me, "So you think you can pull this off? Everyone is counting on you."

"Yup," I said. "Don't worry about it. I got it under control. But can you please get the chemtrail planes ready?"

"How do you suggest you get the water on the plane?" asked Angel.

"*Why don't you let them worry about that?*" I asked.

"How about the water banks?" asked Angel. "How are you going to get the spring connected to the water banks?"

"*I know a company, who could be very discreet,*" I responded mysteriously.

"Okay, as long as it is legit," said Angel. "I am putting my faith in you."

Within a few days, Angel got ahold of a very prestigious company that ran the chemtrail planes. He sent them to San Francisco to get the water at the Golden Gate Bridge Spring to spray water over the farms and national and international forests. At first, people thought it was natural rain, but then they realized it was spring water. People were overcome with joy that they were crying and dancing happily. Life just could not get any better than this!!! They did not know it was the beginning of more good things to come….!!!

It was hard to get ahold of Jonny Luck, my first boyfriend, who was now a Mr. Fix-It. We were playing phone tag for a while before I finally got ahold of him.

Our breakup was for the best; we were moving in different directions ever since he came out of the closet. It was an amiable breakup. We still stayed in contact after so long since our breakup. Although his sibs were accepting of his sexual orientation, his mother was not. She was pretty old-fashioned. (More on that later.)

Jonny was fair-skinned and had flaxen hair. He loved fixing things. Growing up, he was the man of the house after his father walked out on his family, so he basically took care of his brood of six younger brothers and sisters as well as his mother, taking on odd jobs and helping around the house when needed. He finally started his own handyman business, Mr. Fix-It.

His poor mother *still* held a torch for her long-gone husband, hoping he will *one day* come back, but her husband could not take the responsibility of raising a family, so he just up and left. His mother was a high school dropout. She did not know any basic job skills, refusing to go back to school, being from the old school mindset, thinking a woman's place was to stay at home, waiting for the man to 'bring home the bacon,' so to speak. Jonny kept encouraging her to attend night school to get her GED to no avail. He finally gave up on her.

"What is going on, Willie?" asked Jonny when we finally connected with each other. 'Willie' was Jonny's old childhood nickname for me.

"*I have a proposition for you, Jonny*," I said.

"What is it?" he asked. "Is it indecent?"

"*Stop kidding around*," I said.

"Hahaha," said Jonny. "Can't you just take a joke? Why must you take everything so seriously, girlfriend?"

"*Very funny. Seriously, we're in a water crisis, don't ya know? The proposition is this,*" and I launched into a full description of the job. "*I have got a guv'ment job for you, Jonny. I found a spring underneath the Golden Gate Bridge. All you need to do is connect it to* all the water pipes nationally to make water banks for the hospitals and such. And if all goes well, we can take it internationally!" After I had finished, I asked, "Well? Will you take on the job?"

"There is actually a water source in San Francisco!" exclained Jonny incredulously. "That is where the drought first started, being the largest state and all."

"Yes," I sighed heavily. "There is water source in San Francisco. The locals are using like it will never run out."

"How will we connect the water pipes internationally?" Jonny asked.

"I do not know," I said, "We will cross that bridge when we come to it, okay?"

"Sure thing. Oh and Willie, I have been meaning to ask you, does this gig pay well?" Jonny asked.

"Hun, it is a guv'ment job! Of course it pays well!" I exclaimed.

"Just askin'! You don't have to act all peeved off at me! Geez Louise! Let me think about it. I will get back to you in a day or two, okay, girl?" said Jonny.

"Sure," I said, "I will be waiting."

"Talk soon," said Jonny.

"Right back at ya," I replied, hanging up the phone as he also hung up on other end.

Within days, Mr. Fix-It got back to me in a jiffy with his answer. Since Mr. Fix-It had no ball-and-chain to hold him down, he could do it.

"Hey, girl," said Jonny. "Told ya I get back to ya. Okay, since my schedule is pretty much free right now, I guess I can do it."

"Oh, thank you!!! You do not how much that means to

me!!!" I exclaimed. "*I could just* kiss *you!!! You're the* best!!! *You are one in a million!!!*"

"Just how much does this means to you, kid?" asked Jonny.

"*Enough that my boss might give me a raise and a promotion!!!*" I replied, feverish with excitement.

"*One thing I want you to know is do not let the locals*

know that you are working on their spring or else all hell will break loose!" I instructed. "Just work at night, okay?"

"I got this. I will fly out tonight, alright, Willie?" asked Jonny.

"Alright, Jonny," I said. "Just let me know when and where you are when you reach there."

While Jonny was flying out to San Francisco, I told my superior, Angel, that my guy was gonna go out there to check out the situation.

"Hey Angel," I said, knocking on his office door. "May I please come in?"

"Yes, please," Angel called out.

When I had entered, I stood awkwardly around until he invited me to take a seat. "Why don't you please sit down?"

The only other seat was a straight-back chair, so I sat stiffly on the edge of it. "So what is going on?" he asked.

"My guy is flying out to San Francisco right now to assess the situation."

"Did you tell him not to let the locals know? It might stir up trouble," said Angel.

"Do not worry about it," I said. "I had already told him."

"Okay," Angel said. "Thanks for letting me know," as he turned back to his work to make a call. "Can you please close the door when you leave? Thanks."

"I will let you know when he reaches San Francisco," I told him, turning to leave.

"Thank you so much," said Angel.

"You are so very welcome," I said, closing his office door behind me, going back to my cubicle.

While I was on my afternoon break in the break room, I received a call from Jonny in San Francisco. I hurried quickly back to my cubicle, where I can get some privacy.

"Hi Jonny," I said, "Well? Have you found the spring underneath the Golden Gate Bridge?"

"Hello to you, dahling, too," drawled Jonny, "Yup, I am right at ground zero right now. What you request of me is not possible. It is doable. I think it is manageable, but it'll take weeks, possibly months."

"No, hell no! Not months!" I exclaimed.

"Yes, months," Jonny acknowledged. "I know you guys like instant gratification and all, but let's be real: you can't expect me to hook up the water banks from one itty-bitty spring from underneath the Golden Gate Bridge nationally or even internationally. The poor San Franciscans will run out of water even if they said it will last forever."

"*Wait a sec!*" I said, flustered.

"*Don't spring last forever! Isn't that where most bottled water used to come from? Why don't you look some more? When I was there, the spring flowed freely and abundantly.*"

“I think this is the one and only last spring left evah, girlfriend,” said Jonny sadly.

“Is it still flowing? Is there still plenty of water?” I asked.

“Still flowing,” said Jonny. “Plenty, but not enough for national or even international usage. Sorry to rain on your parade.”

“C'mon, what kind of plumber are you?!” I asked

bitterly. "*Why don't you try harder?! Don't be lazybones! I don't want that kind of answer from you, you slacker!*"

"God, you sound like some kind of drill sergeant! Man, oh, man, you are one tough cookie! Alrighty!" relented Jonny. "That's exactly why I open my own business and not work for 'the man.'" With that, he hung up his end of the line, and I also hung up my phone.

I was startled to look up and see my superior, Angel, bearing down on me.

"Great Golly, you scared the bejesus out of me! How long have you been standing there?"

"Long enough to hear your put-downs," Angel replied quietly.

"Oh, it's okay with him; we go waaaaay back," I said.

"But it's not okay with me, with the company," said Angel. "You are on probation till further notice," turning to leave.

"Aw, man," I mumbled, sitting back in my chair, sliding almost to the floor.

"Tough break," said my coworker, Sandy Marshall emphatically, whom I despised and whose cubicle was right next to mine. She was eavesdropping the whole time. "But that's what you get for putting down people."

"Who ask you?" I asked rudely, turning away.

"Well, sorrrrrrrrrrry," Mitchell said, offended, turning back abruptly to her work. "I was just trying to help."

"You can help by staying out of it. Mind your own damn business, you loser," I hissed, trying to keep my temper.

"I'm not the one on probation, so get a grip on yourself," hissed back Mitchell, turning back to her work. "That's the last time I'm helping you out. Next time I ask you for help, don't bother."

"Look, Mitchell, I'm sorry, okay? Buy you lunch sometime? It's just that Angel took my position. I thought when I came back, I will regain my position. Are we friends again?" I said.

"Yeah, I suppose, Willianna" Mitchell said.

Within an hour, Jonny, Mr. Fix-It himself, called me back with news about the spring. "Hey kid," Jonny said. "I got some good news and some bad news. Whatchu want first: the good news or the bad news?"

"Lemme have the good news, Jonny," I said. "I could use some good news."

"Why? What happened?" asked Jonny.

"That's for me to know, and you to find out, buddy," I said.

"Alright," said Jonny. "If that's the way you want it. I am going to hang up now."

"*Wait, don't!*" I yelled, panicking. "*I was just joshing! I can't tell you, but I got in trouble with my boss, okay?*"

"Okay," Jonny. "Alright, the good news is that there is an actually spring. A clear, refreshing spring. Ah, never have I felt water this refreshing in loooooong time yet!"

"Okay, okay, Jon, I know about that already, so spare me the details, alright?" I said. *"So what is the bad news?"*

I waited with abated breath.

"Sorry to break it to you, sugarlips, but, uh, the spring won't last, uh, forever, sweets," said Jonny haltingly, "being the only spring left in the wide world. It is not enough for the United States, never mind the world. It is enough for the State of California for up to 6 months, maybe 3 months, tops. Sorry, sweets." You could tell he was nervous because he was stammering.

"Thank you for letting me know, Mr. Fix-It. Why don't you create water banks for the local hospitals then?" I asked.

"I'll have to get permission from the hospitals, but I think it is doable, girlfriend," said Jonny. "I'll call ya when I do get permission, okay, girl? hang on out there. Hugs and kisses, my dahling, girl," signing off, making a kissing noise on his end of the line.

"*Right back at ya, Mr. Fix-It, chickadee,*" I replied. "*Sorry I can't kiss back; I'm at work now.*

"I understand," said Jonny. "'Bye now, honey. Luv ya."

"*Luv ya too,*" I said.

Our love was like one sibling love another. In this case, Jonny was the older brother, and I was the younger sister.

Jonny was older by a couple of years. Sometimes we fought like cats and dogs, but in the end, we ended up making up. We have known each other since childhood. Jonny always called me Willie. Jonny was my first boyfriend and, I was his first girlfriend. We hung out together till he went off to college. During our childhood, we played in the enchanted forest with the unicorns and centaurs. We made mudpies together. We were inseparable till he left for college, which was a sad day for me. I cried myself to sleep every night. He was my best friend; the one who knew me better than myself. I felt lost without him. I never wanted to enter into a hot and steamy relationship with him because I feared it will endanger our long-lasting friendship.

After he left for college, we talked or Skyped into the night for hours on end about our days. Sometimes, I wished I had made the move to further our relationship, but I am fearful after we break-up, we will never become friends again. Boy, was I wrong!

When I graduated from high school and got into the same college as he did, I decided to make my move. We made a pact that no matter what happens in our relationship, whether we breakup or stay together, we will always, *always* stay together as friends. Our friendship was *that* important to us through and through.

During our college years, we were inseparable just like when we were little. We did everything, and I mean *everything* together! We went to all the college events together. We were one of those rare couples that never fought in college. We stuck by each other through thick and thin, through better and worse. After we had both graduated from college, he came out of the closet to his family. His siblings and I supported him one hundred percent all the way although one important person in his life didn't support his sexual orientation: his mother. I stood by him during this difficult time. We still remained friends, though.

After we hung up, I decided not to tell my boss about my problem. I decided to wait till I gotten the go-ahead from Jonny, then notify my boss.

Meanwhile, I busied myself with menial tasks, tidying up my workspace and doing data entry; stuff I had been putting off while I was in San Francisco. When my boss walked on by, I tried looking totally and absolutely dedicated and diligent, working as studious as possible. But when he scurried by, I took out by Ipod and took out my Emery board to file my nails. Mitchell looked disapprovingly at me. But when I looked her way, she turned away quickly. She didn't want to get want to be at the end of my receiving line. But I saw her.

"Whatchu lookin' at, Mitchell?" I asked in a tight voice

filled with tension to the max. "*Why don't you mind your own damned business?!*"

She pretended not to hear, doing her work, continuing to type away.

"*I know you can hear me,*" I hissed as my boss walked by. "*You were eavesdropping on my phone conversation. Why don't you just leave me alone,*

Mitchell dearest," putting on my

most nauseatingly sweet, syrupy voice

ever.

Made in the USA
Las Vegas, NV
08 February 2024

85474435R00076